Local Colour

LOCAL COLOUR

WILLIAM PLOMER

Foreword by
MARK MITCHELL

ELYSIUM PRESS

Copyright © 1998 The Estate of William Plomer

INTRODUCTION

One afternoon in the summer I was taking a long walk through the part of Rome famous for its antiquarian shops. Along my way, I happened upon a place cluttered with paintings; a place redolent of dust and cigar smoke, like a gentlemen's club. The pictures themselves—mostly somber canvases in darkened gilt frames—confirmed the club atmosphere. There was, however, an amusing portrait of a goat by Filippo Palizzi, a Neapolitan painter, priced at about four thousand dollars. I have thought of it often since, most recently after reading "Local Colour" by William Plomer (his surname rhymes with humor)—a wonderful story, set in Greece, in which a goat acts as something of a silent chorus of one.

"Local Colour" was published in Plomer's third story collection, 1933's *The Child of Queen Victoria*; his his first book to be brought out by Jonathan Cape. (*I Speak of Africa* and *Paper Houses* had been published by Leonard and Virginia Woolf, at the Hogarth Press, in 1927 and 1929 respectively.) Later, in 1949, Plomer included "Local Colour" in a selection of his stories that he put together for Cape under the title *Four Countries*—the four countries being Africa (he was born in South Africa), Japan, Greece and England. Three of the Greek stories in *Four Countries* are explicitly homosexual; besides "Local Colour" and "Nausicaa," the one titled "The Island: An Afternoon in the Life of Costa Zappaglou," which owes a debt to the Guy de Maupassant of "Little Soldier." In his introduction to the volume, Plomer writes that those Greek stories

> are concerned with the pursuit of pleasure in spheres frugal, lazy and corrupt, haunted by the consciousness of ancient glory, and charged with vitality. . . . In three of these stories, I notice, there is a chance impingement upon a Greek scene of individuals from ostensibly more sophisticated levels of civilization, and these sophisticates tend to appear ludicrous, for they lack the dignity, the freedom from fussiness, of the uninhibited and unprivileged persons with whom they come in touch.

Greece was for Plomer what Italy was for E. M. Forster (whose biography he was asked to write), or Germany for Christopher Isherwood, yet like Forster he chose to live in England. At the same time, Plomer —unlike Forster—lived for nearly thirty years with another man: Charles Erdmann, in whose arms he died.

Plomer was one of the most gifted men of English letters in the twentieth century, distinguished equally as a poet, novelist (1952's *Museum Pieces* is a treasure, though *Turbott Wolfe*, from 1925, is perhaps his most famous novel), librettist (Benjamin Britten's opera *Gloriana*—written for the coronation of Elizabeth II— and three "parables for church performance"), biographer (Ali Pasha and Cecil Rhodes), autobiographer, editor (most notably, of the diaries of Victorian clergyman Robert Francis Kilvert), reader (Jonathan Cape) and, again, short story writer. His reputation has dimmed since his death, however, so that while he is the subject of a sympathetic 1989 biography by Peter F. Alexander, at present his work is essentially out of print.

Another picture, this time of Plomer himself: a 1929 portrait by his friend Edward Wolfe (a South African later to become known as "England's Matisse"). The fair and bespectacled (because myopic) writer is sitting in a simple chair, and near a window, with his right leg crossed over his left, his right hand on his right knee, and his left hand on his hip. A brilliant striped carpet and a screen with several panels over which the drapes have been lifted to let in light occupy the rest of the canvas. Plomer, writing of this portrait to Laurens Van der Post, related that the painter Enslin Du Plessis described it as "a mixture of Puck & Buddha!" Du Plessis might have been describing Plomer's work as well as his countenance.

MARK MITCHELL

Upon certain kinds of Nordics the effect of living in Mediterranean countries is the reverse of bracing. The freedom, warmth and glamour of their surroundings begin to sap their intellectual or artistic activity and ambition. They drift into idleness and weaken in will. While constantly talking about what they are going to do and accomplish, they do nothing and make nothing, and at last discover that in gaining liberty and sunshine they have lost purpose and virility. It is a matter of taste and temperament. You can't have everything.

But when the Nordic, young, enterprising and healthy, first finds himself enjoying freedom, warmth, and glamour, the effect upon him is indescribably delightful. He is without responsibilities, he has a susceptible body and an impressionable mind; the sun warms his skin and the blood sings in his veins. Life is full of promise, he is ready for anything, and if anybody asks him if he doesn't feel the heat he says, 'No, I love it.'

Two people in this happy condition were sitting in basket chairs on the veranda of the best hotel in Athens. They were English undergraduates who had come to spend the long vacation in Greece. But they were not sitting there alone. They had a guest—nobody less than Madame Hélène Strouthokámelos.

'Don't you feel the heat?' she said, looking from one to the other.

'Not a bit,' said Grant.

'We love it,' said Spencer.

It *was* extremely hot, all the same. The glare was dazzling. It was just that hour when nothing seems likely ever to cast a shadow again, and the air itself buzzes like a cicada. The young men, neatly dressed in light summer clothing, sat in easy attitudes, but there was much more assurance in their voices than in their feelings. They had brought a letter of introduction to Madame Strouthokámelos and in delivering it had added an invitation to lunch. And here she was in the flesh, and they felt rather shy. Spencer, the English one, was uneasy because he was wearing rather too pretty a tie, which he had bought in Paris, and Madame Strouthokámelos kept glancing at it every now and again as if it offered a clue to his soul. Grant, the Scotch one, had begun looking at the toes of his shoes, and that was always a bad sign with him. Just then an important looking man in a straw hat came up the steps, and catching sight of Madame Strouthokámelos made her an obsequious bow, to which she replied with a cool nod. *Cool*, that was it. It was her coolness that was so disconcerting.

She was neither young nor middle-aged. She had dignity without stiffness, she was handsome, healthy, powerful. There was no powder on her face, she wore no jewellery, and her clothes were simple. She had taken off her little soft hat, just as a girl might have done, with a single gesture and laid it on the table at her side, and now she sat there with her head, most appropriately, against a white marble background. Spencer was facing her, Grant saw her in profile, and if they had been in the presence of Juno herself they could scarcely have been more impressed.

Before meeting her they had tried to imagine what

she would be like, and they had invented a perspiring Levantine matron in black which the sun had faded, with a bluish moustache, bad teeth, and voluble French. And here was Juno at forty, or the Venus of Milo come to life, a woman of noble proportions, with naturally wavy hair, black, becomingly streaked with grey, and drawn back from a smooth forehead, from a face with regular features supported grandly on a firm neck like a cylinder of honey-coloured marble. Her skin was clear and honey-coloured too, and it made the white of her eyes and her fine teeth seem to be ever so slightly tinged with very pale blue. Her strong arms were bare, and her cool dress hung loosely over her firm breasts and clung against her hips and thighs. So much for her appearance. She had a manner to match it.

She had once had a baby—but rather a small one. It often happens with amazonian, mammoth, or merely muscular women that their offspring comes into the world as an embodied protest against size and strength —in fact, the little Strouthokámelos weighed at birth no more than four pounds. It was, however, her husband rather than her child who had mainly disappointed her. Had he been dutiful, she would no doubt have worn him out, but he was casual, and she lost him. Strouthokámelos had been a little too Greek in his nature for her taste—she had been 'finished' in Paris and Vienna, but they hadn't prepared her for what happened. And when it *did* happen she took pains to inform herself about aspects of life, of Greek life, to which she had hitherto paid little attention.

And having been informed, she was resentful. What she could no longer ignore she blamed, frowned upon, or affected not to notice, according to circumstances. And whenever any reflection happened to be cast by foreigners upon the Greeks in general she hastened to proclaim her countrymen's conformity with Christian morality, with the finishing-school view of human nature, failing altogether to remind herself that they are scarcely a European people.

Madame Strouthokámelos was not a fool. She was very much the reverse. Like so many citizens of the lesser European countries she was an excellent linguist, equally at home in English, French, German and Italian. She had read a great deal and was still reading. She was a capable housewife, a born organizer and to some extent a woman of the world. She could stride through thistles in Thessaly, hold her own at the bridge table, make a speech or sack a maid, was a personal friend of the prime minister, and of course was fully equal to the present occasion. She glanced in the direction of the dining-room, and then said:

'Do you specially want us to have lunch here?'

'No,' said Spencer.

'Not if you know of anywhere better,' said Grant.

'Ah, I see you're the practical one,' she said, displaying her classical, milk-blue teeth. 'I don't know about *better*, but hotels are all the same everywhere. I think while you are in Greece you ought to do as the Greeks do. I know a little place down by the sea, towards Vouliagméni, where we could get a nice *Greek* lunch. Do you think you would like that?'

'We should love it,' said Spencer.

'I'm all for local colour,' said Grant.

'Ah, that's just it,' she said. 'If we go there, it will be *Greek*, whereas *this*. . . .' She shrugged her shoulders, but there was a delicious smell of food wafted from the dining-room. 'Then we may as well go at once?' she said, rising to her feet.

Her hosts got up obediently. She was used to obedience.

'You've left your book behind,' she said to Spencer. 'What is it? May I see? Ah, Proust.'

'Do you like Proust?' said Spencer.

'He's very clever, of course, but I don't much care for the atmosphere.'

Spencer popped *Sodome et Gomorrhe* into his pocket.

'And now,' she said, leading the way, 'we'd better get into a taxi.'

The taxis, open touring cars, were lined up under some pepper trees on the opposite side of the road. Madame Strouthokámelos waved away the svelte hotel porter as if he was an insect, led the way, chose a taxi, instructed the driver brusquely, and climbed in. Spencer and Grant exchanged glances and followed. She made them sit one on each side of her, and the taxi drove off, rushing down the Boulevard Amalia towards the sea.

'She doesn't like men,' thought Spencer.

'She despises us,' thought Grant.

'It isn't many miles,' said Madame Strouthokámelos, and began asking them the usual questions about how long they were going to stay, where they were going, and so on.

'I'm afraid we Greeks are rather misunderstood or misrepresented,' she said. 'But there is a wonderful new spirit in the people. The refugees from Asia Minor have increased the population enormously, and have helped to consolidate the national feeling. The younger generation, the Greeks of your age, are manly and patriotic. I think there is great hope for the future.'

'*Manly*,' thought Spencer. 'She's thinking of my tie.'

'What is she getting at?' Grant wondered. 'Is this propaganda?'

It was propaganda.

'So I hope,' she went on, 'that although you'll be here such a short time you'll really be able to get in touch with the people a little and get an idea of what they're really like. That's one reason why I'm taking you to this place for lunch. I don't suppose any foreigner's ever been there before.'

'That's much more interesting than the hotel,' said Grant.

'Much,' said Spencer a little half-heartedly, remembering the smell of the hotel lunch.

'Hotels are *so* much the same everywhere,' she repeated.

They had passed Phaleron, and the conversation turned to Byron. They sped towards Glyphada, along what was then one of the only two decent roads in Greece, and the asphalt was like burnished steel. There was almost no traffic at this time of day. The sea was like a fiery glass and Byron had given place to the Greek language. The road was about to be very bad, when Madame Strouthokámelos, employing that language with great determination, brought the car to a standstill. They all got out, and she waited for her hosts to pay the fare. Then she led the way across a piece of waste land to a little white house by the sea.

There was no path. The way was through loose, burning sand which filled one's shoes. There were some prickly bushes about. They passed a pine tree, sighing to itself. The rays of the sun seemed to be vertical. Presently there was a crazy notice-board decorated with broken fairy-lamps and the inscription Pantheon.

'Here we are,' said Madame Strouthokámelos as if she owned the place.

And immediately a man came out to welcome them. He treated his visitor with deference—she was known to have influence in important circles; her bearing would have demanded respect in any case; and she had brought two young foreigners with her. Well, three lunches meant three profits. He led the trio round to the seaward side of the 'Pantheon'.

'Now, surely this is better than the hotel!' cried Madame Strouthokámelos.

And indeed it was.

A veranda thatched with myrtle branches, and floored with the earth itself, on which stood three round tables covered with coarse but clean tablecloths, and chairs; and only a few yards away, the Aegean sparkling like a million diamonds. There was even a suggestion of a breeze.

The table at the far end was occupied. Four men,

workmen or peasants apparently, were seated there, eating a cheerful meal. Beyond them were some rocks and bushes. At the corner of the house a single plant of maize had grown to a great height. It looked very green and was in flower. Beneath it some fowls were enjoying a dust-bath, and tied to one of the veranda-posts was a goat, recumbent in the shade. With clear yellow eyes which looked as though they missed nothing and saw through everything it watched what was going on. It looked so independent that one could not tell whether it was enjoying what it saw, enjoying a cynical attitude to what it saw, or simply indulging in sheer observation for its own sake.

The proprietor approached Madame Stroutho-kámelos for orders. She took off her little soft hat again with the characteristic sweeping gesture, and then, with a clean, capable hand on which the nails were cut short like a man's she patted her hair, though its wiry waves had not lost their shape.

'There's not much to choose from,' she remarked. 'Of course they weren't expecting us.'

'We leave the choosing to you,' said Grant.

She ordered red mullets, black olives, white bread, a tomato salad, with yaghourt and coffee to follow.

'It sounds marvellous,' said Spencer.

'You'd better taste it first,' she said. 'At least everything here will be fresh.'

The fact that she never wore gloves aided the general impression that she was 'classical' in appearance.

'And what are we going to drink?' she said.

Spencer stole a glance at the other table.

'What are *they* drinking?' he said.

'*Retsina*, probably,' said Madame Strouthokámelos. 'Do you know what that is? White wine with resin in it. It's very nice. Would you like to try some?'

Spencer and Grant said they would, though somebody had told them that it was perfectly revolting.

'I adore the goat,' said Spencer.

'Isn't *adore* rather a strong word?' said Madame Strouthokámelos. 'It seems to me it stinks slightly.' She laughed.

'Exactly what are those people?' said Grant, looking at the other table.

'Oh, just country boys. It's a pity you can't talk to them. Very cheerful, aren't they? And they're really typical.'

They were, indeed, very cheerful, and had just ordered some more wine.

'Would you like to offer them some cigarettes?' said Madame Strouthokámelos. 'They would be very pleased.'

'Would they?' said Grant, and crossed rather shyly to the other table with an open cigarette case. The 'country boys', even more shyly, helped themselves. And Madame Strouthokámelos, leaning forward graciously, addressed them in Greek.

'These are two young Englishmen,' she said, 'visiting Greece for the first time.'

The country boys expressed interest.

'So I've brought them down here to lunch, so that they can see a bit of the *real* Greece.'

The country boys registered approval and pleasure.

'I see you've got a guitar there,' said Madame Strouthtokámelos. 'Won't you sing for these foreigners?'

The country boys laughed and looked at each other and then addressed themselves to one of their number who wore a lilac shirt, urging him to play. He took up the guitar just as the food arrived for the foreigners.

In spite of the heat Spencer and Grant were hungry, and the pleasant atmosphere and the pretty song that was now being sung to the guitar combined to whet their appetites.

'What a delicious lunch,' said Spencer.

'Perfect,' said Grant.

'I'm so glad you're enjoying it,' said Madame Strouthokámelos, and then, turning to the country boys, she suggested another tune for them to play. Her manner was gracious and patronizing and did not go down with them very well. However, the tune she suggested happened to be a favourite with Lilac Shirt, so he soon struck up with it. Drink had made him confident, and vanity made him self-conscious, so he became rather noisy, laughed, and now and then flashed a glance at Spencer and Grant. Madame Strouthokámelos wore an indulgent smile and nodded a gracious acknowledgment.

Conversation turned to the *retsina*. Grant thought it even more disgusting then he had anticipated—it tasted to him like pure turpentine, and he did his best not to make a wry face as he swallowed it. Spencer, who was rather romantic, pretended to himself and to the others that he liked it.

'It has such a nice *piny* sort of taste,' he said. 'But I don't think I could put away quite as much as *they* do—not in the middle of the day, at any rate.'

As he spoke he indicated the country boys, who had opened a fresh lot of wine and were getting very merry.

'Is that what they do every day?' said Grant.

'No, I think they must be celebrating rather a special occasion.'

The proprietor appeared in the doorway, looking genial above his apron. Somebody else had taken the guitar now and was playing a rapid syncopated tune. Lilac Shirt was looking rather flushed. His shirt had come unbuttoned, revealing a lean brown chest, very hairy. He was supporting the head of one of his companions in his lap, and making remarks which surely *must* be ribald. Spencer stole a glance at Madame Strouthokámelos. Yes, sure enough, she was looking at her plate, and a faint frown now marred her rather too regular features. Then Spencer looked at Grant, and Grant looked at Spencer and kicked him under the table, then they both looked at the other table, on which somebody was beating with a spoon just to add to the noise of the guitar and the laughing and the singing.

'They *are* getting gay,' said Spencer, in an affectedly innocent tone of voice.

'They have been drinking a little too much,' said Madame Strouthokámelos with an expression of something like distaste. 'Have you had enough to eat, or shall I order some cheese?'

'Aha,' thought Grant, 'she's trying to hurry us away just when it's beginning to get interesting.' And he said, 'Yes, please. I should like to try the cheese. I expect it's very good here.'

With obvious reluctance Madame Strouthokámelos ordered cheese. The proprietor made a laughing comment on his other visitors, but she did not reply.

At this moment one of the country boys rose to his feet. He was very slender, with lank black hair and rather sleepy-looking eyes. He was going to dance. The others clapped and uttered cries of delight, encouragement and facetiousness. The dancer raised his arms and spread out his hands and began to dance to the guitar. He was skillful and kept excellent time and for a moment it seemed as if Madame Strouthokámelos' slightly disdainful expression might vanish.

'The cheese is excellent,' said Grant.

Spencer lighted a cigarette.

Just then Lilac Shirt rose to his feet, approached the other dancer and clasping one hand round his partner's waist and the other round his loins he called for a tune. Shouts of laughter, and one of the remaining two began again on the guitar. Madame Strouthokámelos frowned once more. The frown was deeper this time.

The tune was a tango. Lilac Shirt proceeded to sway his partner into a caricature of a tango. With absurdly languorous movements they danced, still keeping excellent time with the music. Lilac Shirt's white trousers were, however, a little too tight for really free movement.

'How well they dance,' said Spencer, smiling 'I think

we ought to join in.'

He got another kick under the table.

He then saw that Lilac Shirt's way of holding his partner was perhaps a little too daring, a little too intimate, for the open air, at midday, in public. As the dance continued the goat rose to its feet—as if to get a better view. It stared with its pale amber eyes at the dancers, then turned to look at Madame Stroutho-kámelos—it was a look that spoke volumes, but banned volumes—and then again fastened its keen, glassy, unblinking stare on the dancers.

The guitar-player paused. Lilac Shirt, leaning against his partner who was leaning against one of the veranda posts, embraced him and kissed him on the mouth. This brought loud cheers from the other two. All four of them had forgotten the two foreigners and Madame Strouthokámelos—a fact which made her next words rather wide of the mark.

'They have forgotten themselves,' she said in a tone of disgust. 'They have drunk too much.'

Lilac Shirt's kiss was so prolonged that she averted her eyes and rose abruptly to her feet.

'We had better go,' she said in a quiet and furious voice, and picking up her hat she went round to the landward side of the Pantheon to ask for the bill. Spencer and Grant followed to pay it. Glancing back, they saw Lilac Shirt and his partner disappear behind some rocks a few yards away.

'We live and learn,' said Grant, winking.

As for the goat, it had settled down again, and was quietly chewing the cud. Its yellow eyes were shut for the siesta.

Local Colour
was printed in October of 1998 in an
edition limited to 75 copies. The
typeface is Dante and the paper
is Somerset. You hold
in your hands
copy
38